P9-DGE-631

Mrs. Claus Doesn't Climb Telephone Poles

Want more Bailey School Kids?

Check these out!

#1-46

SUPER SPECIALS **#1-6**

#1-9

And don't miss the...

HOLIDAY SPECIALS

Swamp Monsters Don't Chase Wild Turkeys

Aliens Don't Carve Jack-o'-lanterns

Mrs. Claus Doesn't Climb Telephone Poles

Coming soon...

Leprechauns Don't Play Fetch

Mrs. Claus Doesn't Climb Telephone Poles

by Debbie Dadey
and
Marcia Thornton Jones

illustrated by John Steven Gurney

A
LITTLE APPLE
PAPERBACK

SCHOLASTIC INC.
New York Toronto London Auckland Sydney
Mexico City New Delhi Hong Kong Buenos Aires

To all of Santa's helpers — especially Thelma Thornton, Tillie Cooper, Rita Shelman, Shirley Thornton, and Dick Thornton.
— MTJ
To Sydney and Mason Unger, great neighbors.
— DD

ISBN 0-439-40832-6

12 11 10 9 8 7 6 5 4 3 2 2 3 4 5 6 7/0

Printed in the U.S.A. 40
First Scholastic printing, October 2002

Contents

1

Blizzard of the Century

"Nothing is working," Eddie complained as he tossed his gloves on the snow-covered ground. "I couldn't call Howie last night and the Internet is down. What's going on?"

"It's all this snow," Liza told him. "The weatherman said it was the blizzard of the century. We haven't had this much snow in a hundred years."

Howie, Liza, Eddie, and Melody were gathered under the snow-laden branches of an old oak tree. "It's beautiful," Melody said, looking around at the huge piles of snow that covered everything — even their school.

"This blizzard is good for something," Eddie said with a grin. "School is closed until after Christmas."

Melody threw snow up in the air. The snow sprinkled back down onto her black braids. "We're free!" she cheered. "We can do anything we want!"

"At least until the streets are clear and they open school again," Liza reminded her friends.

"I want to work on my history report," Howie said. "I wonder when the Internet is going to be fixed."

"Forget history until after Christmas," Eddie said. "I want to use the Internet to be the first to squash the alien monster bugs in the Zirlot Space Invaders game."

"Maybe that lady is fixing it right now." Melody pointed to a short, stocky woman in red overalls working high up on a telephone pole. The woman waved to the kids. Liza, Melody, and Howie waved back. Eddie stuck out his tongue and crossed his eyes, but the lady was too far away to see him.

"Be nice," Liza warned. "That lady is working hard!"

"She doesn't look like any telephone repair person I've ever seen," Howie said. "She looks more like she should be baking cookies."

Melody crossed her arms over her chest. "What is that supposed to mean?" she snapped.

Howie shrugged. "Don't get mad at me," he said. "I know women can do anything. It's just that she looks more like my grandmother than a telephone repair person."

Liza giggled. "Grandmothers can climb telephone poles, too, you know."

"I don't care if she's Mother Goose," Eddie complained. "Let's stop talking about her and do something fun. I want to go over to Dedman Hill and go sledding!"

Liza gulped. Dedman Hill was the biggest, slipperiest sledding hill this side of the North Pole. "Why don't we just go home and drink hot chocolate?" Liza suggested. "Or we could make snow

angels." She flopped to the ground, then waved her arms and legs to make an angel.

"No way," Eddie said. "Let's meet at Dedman Hill in fifteen minutes." Eddie grabbed his gloves and followed Melody and Howie.

Liza lay on the ground and groaned. She really didn't want to sled on such a big hill. She started to get up but noticed that the woman on the telephone pole was talking into a receiver. Was it Liza's imagination or did the woman just say, "Ho, ho, ho"?

2

Liza's Wild Ride

"Holy Toledo!" Eddie yelled. "Look at that hill. It's awesome!"

Awesome was not the word that Liza would have chosen. Terrifying was more like it. "Do you think it's safe?" Liza whispered to Melody.

Melody nodded and looked up the huge snow-covered hill. Kids of every size and shape dotted the slope. Some were on sleds and some simply had trashcan lids or pieces of plastic. A few kids tried out snowboards.

"There's that lady again." Howie pointed at a shiny red truck pulling up beside a telephone pole. The woman's tool belt jangled as she hopped out of the driver's seat.

"Duck," Liza called. "She sees us looking at her."

Liza jumped behind a drift of snow, but her friends waved at the woman. "We don't have to hide," Eddie said. "We're not doing anything wrong."

Liza's face turned red. She stood up as the woman introduced herself. "Greetings," the woman said. She was dressed entirely in red. Even her boots, cap, and mittens were red. "My name is Joy. Those are some nice sleds you have. Of course, my favorite is the QT-10."

Melody's eyes lit up. "I saw that at the hardware store. It's the best!"

"It's also very expensive," Howie told her. "My mother said she'd buy a house in Tahiti before she'd buy a sled that cost that much."

Joy nodded. "It is expensive," she said. "I must admit that the L-B56 is pretty good, too, and it's a lot cheaper."

"How do you know so much about sleds?" Eddie asked.

The lady put her hand over her mouth. “Oops, I’d better get to work.” She hustled away and climbed the telephone pole without saying another word.

“I wonder if she has the phone lines fixed yet,” Howie said.

“We’ve wasted enough time blabbing,” Eddie snapped. “I came to go sledding. Who’s ready?”

Liza stared down at her boots. Eddie grabbed her arm and pulled. “Come on, Liza,” Eddie said. “I’ll race you.”

Liza’s face turned whiter than the snow. “I . . . I . . . I think I’ll just watch for a while,” she stammered.

Eddie took one look at Liza and started teasing her. “Liza’s scared. Liza’s a wimp.”

“Cut it out,” Melody told Eddie. “Liza doesn’t have to go down the hill if she doesn’t want to.”

Eddie shrugged. “She’ll miss out on all the fun if she doesn’t.”

Liza watched while Melody, Howie,

and Eddie pulled their sleds up the steep hill. They stood in line and waited for their turn. Then, one at a time, her friends zoomed down.

"Ya-hoo!" Howie screamed.

"Coooooool!" Melody yelled.

"Holy Toledo!" Eddie hollered.

Liza had to admit it did look fun — a lot more fun than standing at the bottom watching everyone else. She took a deep breath and trudged up the hill beside Melody.

"You don't have to do this," Melody told Liza.

"I want to," Liza said, even though her stomach was doing a dance.

"One, two, three, go!" Eddie shouted. Before Liza could change her mind, Eddie shoved her sled with a snow-crusted boot. Then he hopped on his sled and zoomed down alongside her. "I'm going to beat you!" Eddie screamed into the rushing wind.

Liza wasn't the least bit interested in

winning a downhill race against Eddie. She was too worried about surviving the trip. Liza closed her eyes as she whisked down the hill. "Helpppppppppp!" she screamed.

Liza opened her eyes in time to see Eddie slip behind her. Everything was a blur as she whipped along. Finally, she reached the bottom of the hill and coasted to a stop.

Liza stood up with trembling knees and looked around for her friends. Eddie had stopped halfway up the hill and lots of other kids were close to him. She was the only one to make it all the way to the bottom.

At the top of the hill, Melody put her hands around her mouth and yelled, "Way to go, Liza! You won! You won!"

Eddie wasn't cheering. He stood up and kicked his sled. He didn't even look at Liza, but pushed his way back up the hill and to the front of the line.

"Hey," Melody told Eddie. "Just because

Liza went farther than you, doesn't mean you have to get mad."

"I'm not mad," Eddie snapped. "And I don't have to listen to you — or to anyone else. I can do whatever I want."

Liza climbed to the top of the slope and noticed that Joy was now on the telephone pole just behind a nearby spruce tree. Liza could hear Joy's tools jangling, but that wasn't all she heard. Liza was sure she heard Joy say "ho, ho, ho" into a phone line.

Liza pulled Melody away from the line of kids. Howie and Eddie came over to see what was going on. "I just heard Joy say 'ho, ho, ho,'" Liza told them. "She said it before, too."

Eddie rolled his eyes. "Big deal. Anyone can say 'ho, ho, ho.' See? Ho, ho, ho, ho," he said, just to prove his point.

Liza ignored Eddie. "Isn't it strange how the telephone lady just appeared after the big blizzard?" she said. "It's almost like she *blew* into town."

Melody patted Liza's shoulder. "I think we need to get you out of the cold. You're starting to sound a little flaky."

"How about we *blow* into Burger Doodle for some hot chocolate?" Howie suggested. "My hands are freezing."

Eddie nodded. "Let's sled down one more time first."

"Not me," Liza said. "One wild ride a day is enough. I'm walking down."

"What?" Eddie snapped. "You have to race me again."

"Not today," Liza said.

Eddie didn't want to give up. "Then when?" he asked.

Liza rubbed her hands together to keep them warm. "Next Saturday."

"That's Christmas Eve," Eddie complained. "It's too far away!"

Liza didn't answer Eddie. She started walking down the hill. Secretly she hoped all the snow would melt before next Saturday. It had been exciting to sled down Dedman Hill once, but she wasn't sure she ever wanted to try it again.

"Wait a minute!" Eddie yelled. He ran to catch up with Liza and tripped in the thick snow. Instead of sledding down the hill, Eddie slid down on the seat of his pants. "Ahhhhh!" he screamed.

Melody giggled. "Now, *that's* one wild ride."

3

Rotten Fruitcake

As soon as Eddie slid to a stop he was off and running. "Last one to Burger Doodle is a rotten fruitcake!" he screamed over his shoulder.

"Too late!" Melody yelled, taking off after him. "You're already the most rotten fruitcake of all!"

Melody was almost even with Eddie when he cut in front of her, forcing her to stumble into a pile of snow. "No fair!" Melody hollered as Eddie zipped around a corner toward Burger Doodle.

"All's fair in racing and war!" Eddie called back.

Melody stomped in a slush puddle. "That Eddie can be a real pain in the neck," she said when Howie and Liza

finally caught up to her. "He wouldn't even wait for his friends!"

"You didn't wait for us, either," Howie pointed out.

Melody didn't answer. She couldn't. Eddie popped around the corner and lobbed a snowball at her. It slammed right into Melody's knees. Snow dribbled down inside her boot.

"I'll get you for that!" Melody shouted. Off she ran, chasing Eddie right to the door of Burger Doodle Restaurant. Bells over the door jangled as Melody, Liza, and Howie followed Eddie inside.

"Beat you!" Eddie said with a grin as he rushed to be first in line.

"You cheated," Melody told him. "It doesn't count."

Eddie didn't pay any attention to Melody. As soon as he got his hot chocolate and a giant chocolate chip cookie, Eddie hurried across the restaurant so he could be the first to slide into a booth. When his friends were seated, he stuffed the entire cookie in his mouth. "I beat everyone," he said, only he was hard to understand because his mouth was full of cookie crumbs.

Liza rolled her eyes. Howie ignored him. Melody pointed her finger at Eddie's nose. "You are being very rude," she told him.

Liza nodded. "Everything doesn't have to be a race, you know."

"You're just saying that because you're a slowpoke," Eddie told Liza. "And I plan to prove it next Saturday when we race down Dedman Hill. Too bad I don't have a QT-10 or an L-B56."

"Those new sleds could be dangerous," Liza said after taking a sip of hot chocolate. "I think racing down Dedman Hill is dangerous."

"Liza's right," Howie said. "Maybe racing isn't such a good idea."

Melody glared at Eddie. "If Liza doesn't want to race, she doesn't have to."

Eddie wadded up a napkin and threw it at Melody. "Quit being such a goody-goody," he said. The napkin missed Melody, sailing over her head and right into the path of a short man dressed entirely in green.

"Pardon me," the man said. He quickly bent down, picked up the napkin, and handed it back to Eddie.

"You almost beaned a perfect stranger," Melody snapped at Eddie when the man walked away. "You're getting on everyone's nerves."

"He's not a stranger," Liza said softly. "I know him from somewhere. I just can't remember where."

Melody and Eddie were too busy bickering to hear her. Liza leaned around the corner of the booth and watched the short man as he made his way around tables and chairs to the back of the dining room. Liza gasped when she saw where he was heading.

"What's wrong?" Howie asked.

"That man," she said. "He's here to talk to Joy."

There, in the back booth, sat the woman who had been working on the telephone lines. She slowly stirred a cup of hot cider with a candy cane.

"So?" Eddie asked. "Who cares?" He took a sip of hot chocolate and ended up with a big brown mustache.

"Shh," Liza said. "I wonder what they're talking about."

"Only one way to find out," Eddie said. He slid down in his seat and crawled out from under the table. "Follow me," he whispered.

"Eddie," Melody warned, "it's not nice to spy on people."

Eddie didn't hear her. He was already halfway across the dining room. "We better go with him to make sure he doesn't cause any trouble," Liza said. She slid out of the booth. Howie looked at Melody and shrugged before following his two friends. Melody sighed. Sitting all alone in the booth didn't sound like much fun at all. She followed her friends.

Eddie had plopped down in the booth right behind Joy and the little man dressed in green. Liza, Howie, and Melody quietly sat down next to Eddie.

"Ho, ho, ho," Joy said to the little man. Only Joy didn't sound happy at all.

"Everyone at the shop is worried," the man said. "Will you tell me what happened?"

Joy took a deep breath. "I'm going to level with you. S.C. made me mad. He doesn't even remember to say good morning half the time. He's always busy, busy, busy. Sure, he's a jolly old soul, but sometimes I wish he would stop all that belly laughing and notice the work I've been doing. After all, if it wasn't for me, he wouldn't have his lists organized on the computer. And who keeps the workers'

BURGER
DOODLE

schedule straight? Me, that's who. But, do I get any credit? No! Not even a thank-you. Nobody appreciates a single thing I do. Especially S.C.!"

"Haven't we seen that man somewhere before?" Liza whispered to her friends.

Howie quickly peeked over the top of the booth. "He does look familiar," he agreed.

"I need time away," Joy was saying. "Besides, S.C. is so busy he'll never miss me."

"That's not true," the man in green said. "He misses you. Everyone does. Production is down and no one feels like working. We won't meet our deadline without you. You must fly home before it's too late!"

Joy pulled a big red hanky from the pocket of her overalls and blotted her eyes. "If S.C. really misses me, then he'll come get me himself, Eli," she said.

Just then, Liza let out a scream that brought the entire restaurant to a complete standstill.

4

Abominable Snowman

All eyes turned to the booth where the four kids sat. The other customers looked at the kids for a full thirteen seconds. Then they turned back to their food.

"Whew," Howie said. "That was a close call."

"Let me tell you something about the spying business," Eddie said under his breath. "It's a good idea not to scream or yell or do dances on tables. That tends to blow your cover."

Liza leaned toward the center of the table and waited for her friends to huddle close. "Didn't you hear what Joy called that man in green?" Liza whispered. "Eli!"

"So?" Melody and Howie asked at the same time.

Liza's eyes were wide as she helped them remember. "Eli was the same man we saw talking to that janitor we had for a while. Remember? The janitor who turned out to be Santa Claus."

"We never proved that janitor was really Santa," Howie pointed out.

"Howie is right," Melody said. "He was probably just a fat man who was good with a mop."

"He was Santa Claus," Liza said. "I'm sure of it. And Eli is Santa's helper. That means Joy must be from the North Pole, too!"

Eddie looked at Liza, crossed his eyes, and put two straws in his mouth for fangs. "Yes, and I'm the Abominable Snowman," he said with a goofy grin.

"You're half right." Melody giggled. "You're definitely abominable!"

Liza was ready to argue, but a long shadow suddenly blocked the sun shining through the restaurant's windows. Liza shivered and looked right up into

Joy's blue eyes. The kids had been so busy talking they hadn't noticed that Eli had left the restaurant.

"Well, I see you four have come in off the slopes," Joy said. "How about a candy cane?"

"All right," Eddie cheered, reaching for the candy.

"Thank you, but we aren't allowed to take candy from strangers," Liza said politely, pulling Eddie's hand away.

Joy put her hands to her rosy cheeks. "Oh, you are so right! Up north, everyone knows me."

"We saw you working on the telephone poles," Howie said. "Do you like it?"

Eddie stood up on his seat so he towered over his friends. "Climbing poles would be fun. Have you ever tried tying a rope to the top for a giant swing?"

Joy giggled and her blue eyes sparkled. "Oh, my. That wouldn't be a smart thing to do, now would it?"

Eddie opened his mouth to answer but

snapped it shut. Joy had tricked him into being speechless.

"Climbing poles is fun, but it's also hard work," Joy said, not seeming to notice Eddie's silence. "I'm pretty good at it, if I do say so myself. I've been making and fixing things for as long as I can remember."

"I wish I could fix things," Eddie blurted. "Then maybe I could fix my favorite toy."

Joy clapped her hands. "I do enjoy toys, even though I haven't been a child for centuries. What is your favorite toy?"

Eddie puffed out his chest. "It's a giant Bug Squasher action figure from the Planet Zirlot. It has twelve legs and laser beams for eyes. I broke it by accident last week."

"I know all about Bug Squashers from Zirlot," Joy said. "I especially like the way their heads twirl in circles. If you like those, then I bet you'd really enjoy the hottest new action figure — the new, improved, super-duper Bug Squasher Z-Model."

Eddie jumped out of his seat. "Of course I would. I really want one. Every kid wants one. I bet I get a Z-Model for Christmas."

Joy's eyes sparkled. "That all depends, now doesn't it?" she said softly.

"Joy is right. You better not get your hopes up," Melody said, patting Eddie on the arm. "They've been sold out for weeks."

"The only person who could get a Z-Model this close to Christmas is Santa Claus himself," Howie added.

Liza nodded. "Of course Santa could get one. Santa can do anything, can't he?"

Joy cleared her throat and her eyes lost their sparkle. She looked at the four friends sitting in the booth. Then, without another word, Joy turned and ran out of Burger Doodle. The bells over the door jingled long after she was gone.

5

Everywhere

"No," the clerk told Eddie. "We sold out of that toy at least two months ago."

"Rats," Eddie said. "I've been to every place in town and it's the same story."

The kids were in the toy department of Dover's Department Store. It was the day after they had been sledding. Snow still coated the streets and sidewalks. "I told you they were sold out," Melody said to Eddie. Howie ignored all his friends. He was busy looking at a microscope. Howie wanted to be a doctor someday and was always interested in anything having to do with medicine or science.

The clerk shrugged his shoulders and walked away. "Maybe you could try asking Santa."

"Or Mrs. Claus," Melody said with a giggle.

"Look," Liza said, interrupting her friends. The kids turned around to see Joy talking with another salesclerk.

"Now, personally," Joy was saying, "I wouldn't recommend the Suzy Kellogg Egg Fryer for anyone under five, but the Mickey Flip-Flop Fryer is safe for any age."

The clerk nodded and asked, "What do you think about the Deluxe Doggy Doo-Doo Maker?"

Joy giggled. "That's the silliest toy I've ever seen. I hope parents aren't crazy enough to buy it for their little darlings."

The clerk laughed while Joy threw her head back and belted out a loud, "Ho, ho, ho."

Later that week, the kids were at the Bonsai Bakery. Melody had to pick up a cake because her aunt was coming for Christmas Eve dinner. Nobody was be-

MICKY
FLIP FLOP
FRYER
Suzy Kellogg
EGG FRYER
DELUXE
DOGGIE

hind the counter, so Eddie rang the bell for service. *Ring. Ring. Ring.* "Come on," Eddie snapped. "We don't have all day."

"Eddie," Liza told him. "You should have more patience."

"Patience, smatience," Eddie said. "I have things to do."

Howie nodded. "Yeah, like our history report."

Eddie rolled his eyes. History and bakeries were definitely not what he had in mind, but he couldn't help drooling as he stared at the sugar cookies and butterscotch drops behind the counter.

"There's the problem," Melody said. Through the doorway, the kids saw Joy chatting with the owner.

"That lady is everywhere," Eddie snapped. "Why doesn't she climb back up a telephone pole and stay there?"

"Shh," Liza said. "Let's listen."

"Yes," Joy was saying. "Five cups of sugar and not one bit more. Those cookies will be perfect."

That wasn't the last time the kids saw Joy that week. When the kids were at the mall with Eddie's grandmother, they saw Joy in Fred Barbo's Sportarama. "That lady is starting to give me the creeps," Melody said.

"She's everywhere," Howie agreed.

"What's she up to now?" Liza asked.

"Come on," Eddie said. "Let's find out."

The kids sneaked up behind a big canoe to listen. "This is a good coat," Joy told a customer.

"Do you work here?" the man asked.

"Oh, heavens no," Joy said. "But where I come from it's very cold. I know a good coat when I see one. I've made plenty in my day."

The customer nodded and walked away with the coat. Liza stood up and waved to Joy. "Greetings," Joy said, holding up a scarf. "What a pleasure to see you."

"Are you shopping for your husband?"

Liza asked. Howie, Melody, and Eddie stood up beside the canoe.

"I do have half a mind to get a scarf for my husband. He's always so busy getting presents for everyone else, going over his lists, and checking them twice. A scarf would be the perfect thing for him. I can never get him to wear one and his nose stays as red as a cherry gumdrop," Joy said.

"You must really care about your husband to worry about his nose," Howie said.

"Of course I care about him," Joy said. "But do you think he'd give one thought about my nose? Of course not. He's too busy for that." Joy folded the scarf and plopped it back on the shelf. "Excuse me, children. I want to talk to this clerk about those new sleds."

Liza stared at Joy as she walked away. Something about what Joy said bothered Liza. She just couldn't figure out what it was.

6

The North Pole

"You have to come with me," Liza told her friends on the morning of Christmas Eve. They were standing under the oak tree, trying to warm their hands. The wind whistled through the tree branches and little snowflakes danced in the air.

"No way," Eddie snapped. "You promised me we'd have a sled race today and you're not going to get out of it."

Liza gulped. She didn't really want to race down that huge hill again, and right now she had more important things on her mind. She'd been thinking about Joy all week. "I'll go sledding right after we do this one thing," she told her friends. "I promise."

"Oh, let's just go with her," Melody said. "She won't stop asking until we do."

Howie shrugged. "I'll go."

Earlier, on her way to the oak tree, Liza had seen Joy up a telephone pole at the corner of Main and Forest Lane. The kids got to the corner just in time to see Joy walking away. "Come on," Liza whispered. "We don't want to lose her."

Eddie grumbled. "I can't believe I'm chasing a grandma down the street when I could be sledding."

"Eddie," Liza said softly. "This is important." The kids followed Joy down Main Street and past Howie's house. Joy turned off Main Street onto a little gravel road. The street sign said SNOWFLAKE LANE.

"I've never been this way before," Howie said. "I wonder what's down here." Howie didn't have to wonder for long. The kids passed a grove of towering pine trees and came into a clearing just in time to see Joy enter a small cottage.

"Oh, it's adorable," Melody said.

"It looks like the house from *Hansel and Gretel,*" Liza admitted.

Eddie rubbed his stomach and mumbled, "I wonder if I can eat it."

"Only if you want to get electrocuted," Howie pointed out. "Look at all those lights."

Twinkling Christmas lights outlined the roof, the door, and every window. All around the house, spruce trees and bushes glittered with lights and ornaments. Bright red-and-white candy canes lined the brick sidewalk. A giant snowman smiled down at the kids from the roof.

Eddie laughed out loud. "This house looks like something from the North Pole. I wish my dad didn't travel so much. Then he'd have time to put up lights like this."

Liza stared at Eddie. "What did you say?" she asked.

"I said, I wish my dad would put up Christmas lights," Eddie said.

Liza shook her head. "No, what else did you say?"

Eddie was tired of looking at lights. "Stop wasting time," he said. "You promised you'd sled today. So let's get going." Eddie jogged away without waiting for an answer.

Liza took one more look at the little cottage on Snowflake Lane. There was something very mysterious about it. She just wished she could figure out what it was. Unfortunately, she didn't have time to think. Right now, she had to risk her life on Dedman Hill.

7

The Abominable Snowman Strikes Again

As usual, Eddie beat his friends to Dedman Hill. He leaned his sled against a tree at the base of the hill and hoisted himself up to a low branch. Eddie had a perfect view of all the action.

Eddie wasn't the only one with a good view. Joy was high up a nearby telephone pole. Her tool belt jangled as she perched near the top and worked on the lines.

Several kids were slowly climbing the steep slope. A small boy at the top peered over the edge of the hill, then took a step back in fear. Eddie would never be afraid to zip down the slope. He couldn't wait to show every kid in Bailey City how fast he could go. Especially Liza.

As soon as Howie, Liza, and Melody were under Eddie's tree, he roared, "The Abominable Snowman strikes again!" Then Eddie shook the tree limb. An avalanche of snow fell right on his friends' heads.

"Eddie, you are worse than the Abominable Snowman," Melody said, shaking snow from her braids.

Liza giggled and wiped snow from Howie's back. "I bet the Abominable Snowman would run from Eddie."

"He couldn't outrun me and my superslide sled," Eddie bragged. "It can go faster than a snow monster and anyone else on this hill. I bet I can ride faster than Santa's sleigh!"

Melody rolled her eyes. "Bragging doesn't make it true," she told Eddie. "It only means you're the biggest pest on this hill."

Eddie jumped down and faced Melody, nose to nose. "You don't think I'm the fastest one here?"

Melody took one step back. "I know you're not the fastest because Liza beat you last week," she told Eddie. "You might as well face it. Liza is faster than you."

Eddie's face turned red, and it wasn't just from the cold wind. "I wasn't trying to win that day!" Eddie said before stomping up the hill.

"Eddie needs to learn that winning isn't everything," Melody said. "And I'm just the one to teach him. Let's go!"

The three friends followed Eddie. Their boots sunk deep in the snow and their breath made tiny white clouds. As soon as they reached the top, Eddie shoved aside two kids to get to the front of the line.

"Wait your turn," Melody said.

"I don't have time to wait," Eddie snapped. "This hill has my name on it."

"That's it!" Melody snapped. "I've had enough of your abominable behavior." Melody was so mad, she stomped away.

Eddie didn't care. He was determined

to prove that he had the fastest sled on the hill. He dropped his sled at the top of the hill. Then he stood on top of it.

"Eddie!" Liza yelped. "Get down before you hurt yourself!"

Eddie grinned and held his hands high over his head. "I am the future gold-medal winner of the Dedman Hill Olympics!" he hollered.

Unfortunately, the sled started moving through the snow while he was in the middle of his victory cheer.

"Watch out!" Howie warned.

Too late. The sled slipped out from under Eddie. He fell into a deep pile of snow. His sled zoomed down the hill without him. "NOOOOOOOOOO!" Eddie screamed as his sled headed straight for the tree at the bottom of the hill. It smacked into the tree and broke into three pieces.

"My sled! My sled!" Eddie cried out. "No fair!"

Melody shook her hand in Eddie's

direction. "You're lucky you didn't crack your head," she told him.

Howie helped Eddie out of the snow-drift. He was covered in snow from the top of his curly red hair to the bottom of his black boots.

"Now you really do look like the Abominable Snowman," Liza said with a giggle.

"It's not funny," Eddie said. "My sled's broken into smithereens. This is the worst Christmas Eve ever!"

Eddie sat on the ground and slid all the way down the hill on the seat of his pants. Howie and Melody zipped by him on their sleds. Liza peered down the hill after her friends. Down, down, down they went. The longer they slid, the more her stomach tumbled. She decided to walk down the hill instead of sliding.

Just as Liza reached the bottom, Joy shimmied down a nearby telephone pole to join the kids. They were trying to put Eddie's sled back together again.

"Looks like you had an accident," Joy said to Eddie.

"It wasn't my fault," Eddie told her, holding up a piece of his sled. "It just took off on its own. Now my sled is ruined."

Joy kneeled down to examine the damage. "Well, now," she said. "I wouldn't say it's ruined. It just needs a few screws tightened." Joy whipped a screwdriver from her belt and bent over the sled. She worked so fast, Liza had a hard time following Joy's hands. "There you go," Joy said suddenly. "All fixed."

"Wow!" Eddie said with a low whistle. "I was sure this sled was toast, but you made it look good as new!"

"My husband and I can fix just about anything," Joy said. "We've had lots of practice."

"What kind of job does your husband have?" Melody asked.

Joy laughed from deep in her belly. "You might say he's into toys," she said.

Then her smile faded. "They're his whole life. Even more important than me."

"How can I ever thank you?" Eddie asked as he ran his hands over his sled. For some reason, it looked shinier than before. "I'll do anything!"

"I hope you mean that," Joy said. "Because I know just the thing."

8

Magic

Joy smiled and patted Eddie on the head. “This is what you must do for me. From now on, I want you to be more careful. Just think how your family would feel if you got hurt.”

Eddie thought for a moment. Then he nodded. “My grandmother would be upset if something happened to me. Who would she bake cookies for? Who would she buy toys for? Who would she read to at night?”

Melody sighed. “I would miss my mom and dad if I had to be away from them for a while. They would miss me, too.”

“My family plays board games and cards every Friday night,” Liza said. “I would miss that.”

Howie nodded. “I would miss the way

my dad can turn doing the dishes into a science experiment."

Joy put her hand over her heart. Tears puddled in her blue eyes. "I must admit, all this talk of family makes me miss my husband."

"Where is your husband?" Howie asked.

"He's up north," she told him. "And all this beautiful snow reminds me of our little cottage nestled amidst the snowdrifts and glaciers."

The more Joy talked, the quieter Liza became. Not Eddie. He grew more restless. He stomped his foot, splattering them all with snow.

"All this snow reminds me of the race that's waiting for me at the top," Eddie interrupted. Then he looked right at Liza. "It's now or never," he said. "Get your sled, Liza. We have a date with Dedman Hill!"

Liza's mouth was suddenly dry. She tried to swallow. Her knees started shaking and she sat down hard in the snow.

"Are you too chicken?" Eddie asked.

"Leave her alone," Melody warned. "She doesn't have to sled down Dedman Hill if she doesn't want to."

Joy looked up at the top of the hill. Then she looked down at Liza. "I used to be quite a sledder back in my day," Joy said. "I have a great idea. How about if you and I go down together?"

"That might make it easier," Liza admitted. "Would you mind?"

"Mind? Of course not. I think it sounds absolutely marvelous."

Marvelous was putting it mildly. At the top of the hill, Joy hopped on the sled behind Liza and pushed off. Liza's sled quickly became a blur. They went so fast it looked like the sled's runners flew over the top of the snow. Liza didn't feel the least bit scared with Joy behind her.

Eddie stomped his feet and huffed into the cold air. "No fair. I want to go that fast."

Eddie didn't need to be mad. As soon

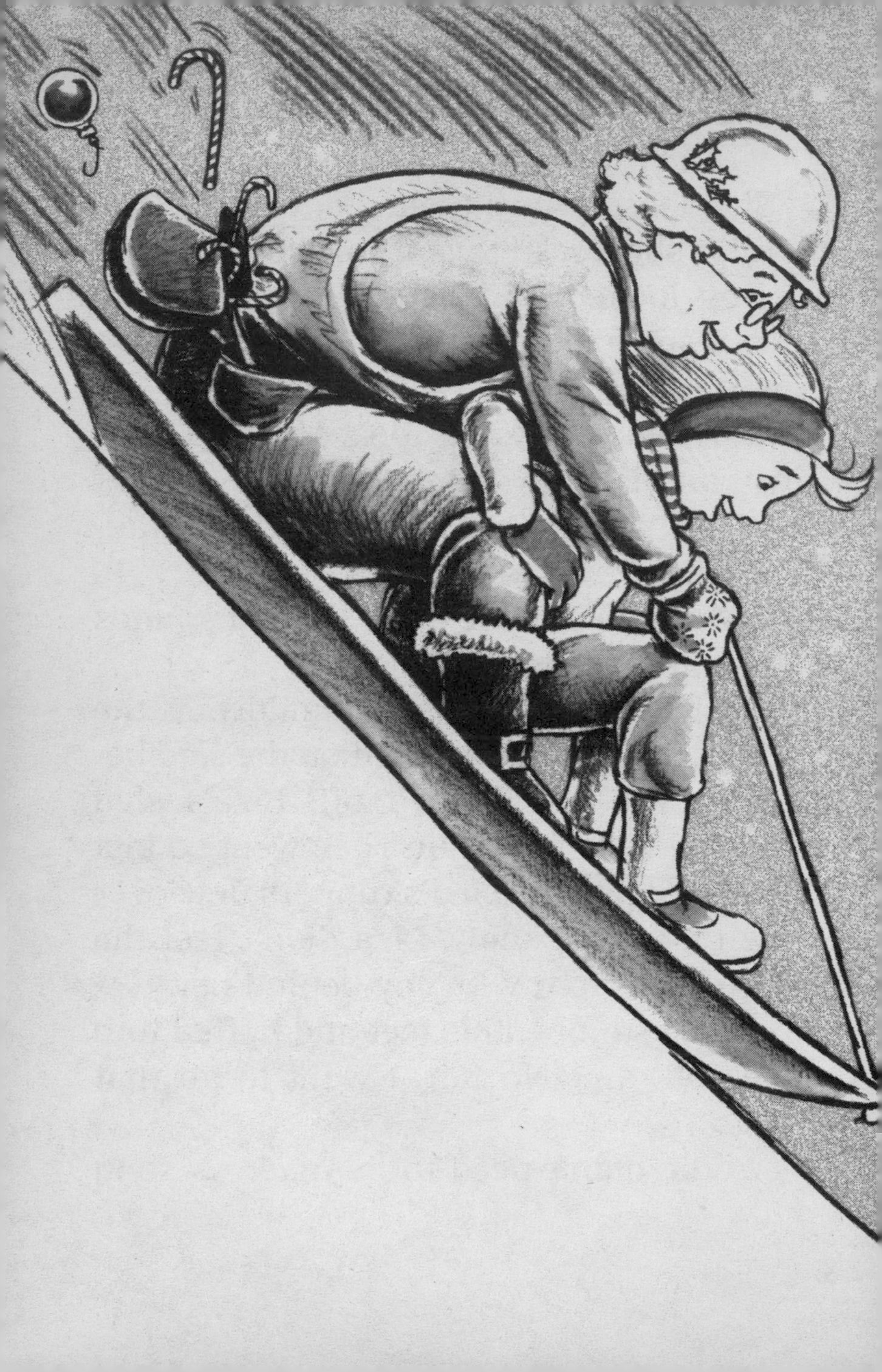

as Joy climbed to the top of the hill, she hopped on Eddie's sled. Together, Joy and Eddie flew down the steep slope. In fact, Joy rode with everyone.

"Wow," Melody said. "Every sled Joy rides seems to soar over the snow."

Howie's ears were tipped in red from the cold. He pulled his hat down over them. "It's almost like winter magic," he said.

Liza's eyes widened and her face turned as white as the snow on her mittens. "What did you say?" Liza asked.

"It just seems odd that the sleds go so fast when she's on them," Howie explained.

"Exactly," Liza said. She grabbed Howie's and Melody's coat sleeves and pulled them away from the rest of the kids on the hill. Eddie noticed his friends whispering. He hated the idea of losing his place in line, but he hated being left out of a secret even more. He scuffed through the snow to see what they were talking about.

"There's something very unusual about Joy," Liza was saying.

Eddie nodded. "She's fun," he said. "She hasn't forgotten how to play."

"That's because," Liza said slowly, "Joy has had lots of practice."

Melody pulled Liza's hat down over her ears. "Have your brains frozen?" she asked. "You're not making any sense."

Liza pushed Melody's hand away from her hat. "I'm making perfect sense. Joy has had lots of practice playing because she is the one and only Mrs. Santa Claus!"

Melody giggled. Howie smiled. Eddie plopped down in the snow and laughed out loud. "I'm pretty sure Santa's wife has better things to do than fix telephone wires," Eddie said.

"Eddie's right," Howie said. "The North Pole is far away. Why would Mrs. Claus want to vacation in Bailey City?"

"After all," Melody added, "I'm pretty

sure Mrs. Claus doesn't climb telephone poles."

"You have to believe me," Liza said. "I have it all figured out. Santa and Joy had a misunderstanding. It's up to us to get them back together. If we don't, something terrible might happen!"

9

Snowball Fight of the Century

"Who cares?" Eddie told Liza.

Howie rubbed his gloves together to stay warm and nodded. "Eddie has a point. Even if Joy is the one and only Mrs. Claus, what difference would it make to us?"

Liza stomped her foot and looked at Eddie. "What if Joy tells Santa's elves everything that happens in Bailey City, including who's naughty or nice?"

"I'm not worried," Eddie said. "I'm not naughty."

Howie laughed and Liza shook her head. "You *should* be worried," Liza told Eddie.

"You're not exactly nice all the time," Melody pointed out.

"Eddie knows how to be good," Howie said in defense of his friend.

Liza nodded. "Good at trouble," she added.

"No," Eddie argued. "This city would be boring without me because I'm good at stirring up excitement. And that's exactly what I plan to do right now." Eddie scooped up a big snowball and tossed it at Liza. Soon he was throwing snowballs at everyone on the hill.

"Eddie, will you please listen to me?" Liza yelled as she ducked a snowball.

"I'm tired of listening," Eddie said. "We're kids. We're supposed to have fun!"

A girl named Becky tossed a big snowball at Eddie and hit him right on the mouth. Eddie spit out snow and shouted, "Look out! It's the snowball fight of the century!" He tossed snowballs like a catapult. Kids dived onto the snow-covered ground to avoid getting hit.

"Eddie, quit acting so crazy," Melody yelled, but Eddie didn't listen. When a

kid named Huey wasn't looking, Eddie put ice down Huey's shirt.

Melody tried to grab Eddie's coat to stop him, but he put snow in a kindergartner's mitten anyway. "Now that was downright mean," Melody snapped.

"I'm just having fun," Eddie said. "You need to stop being so grouchy."

"And you need to be nicer," Melody said as she ducked a snowball. Eddie didn't quit throwing snowballs, so Melody gave up trying to stop him. In fact, Melody threw a few snowballs of her own. Kids all over the top of Dedman Hill joined in the snowball fight.

Eddie was having a great time. What he didn't know was that Joy was watching. Liza knew. She had ducked behind a snow-laden spruce tree to avoid one of Eddie's snowballs. That's when Liza noticed Joy watching every snowball Eddie lobbed into the air. Joy shook her head each time Eddie did something not so nice.

“I have to tell Eli about this,” Liza overheard Joy mutter out loud. With a jingle of her tool belt, she shimmied up a nearby telephone pole, whipped out her headset, and tapped into the telephone line.

“Ho, ho, ho,” Joy said loud enough for Liza to hear. “Eli, there’s something you should know before you leave tonight. Something important!”

10

Hot

After all that snowball throwing, Eddie needed a rest. "Let's head to Burger Doodle!" he shouted.

A huge group of kids followed Eddie down Forest Lane. They threw a few snowballs along the way but calmed down as they went inside Burger Doodle. "I want hot chocolate," Eddie told Skip, the counter worker.

"I'd like a Doodlegum Shake, please," Liza said. Melody and Howie got shakes, too. After the friends had their drinks, they headed to a booth against the back wall. Liza told her friends what she had overheard.

"Big deal," Eddie said. "It's not against the law to make a phone call, even if it is from the top of a pole."

Eddie took a big gulp of his hot chocolate and immediately spit it out all over the table. "Eddie," Melody shrieked. "That's disgusting." Howie grabbed some napkins and wiped up the table.

Eddie stuck out his tongue and fanned it. "Hot!" he whined. "My tongue is on fire!"

Liza giggled and gave Eddie a sip of her cold shake. "That's why it's called HOT chocolate," she said.

When Eddie had finally calmed down, Liza got serious. "We have to help Santa and Joy make up," she said. "If we don't, Santa might be too sad to deliver presents. There won't be a single toy under our trees tomorrow."

Howie shrugged. "I'm not sure Joy is Mrs. Claus, but even if she isn't, it would be nice to help her make up with her husband."

"It would be romantic," Melody agreed.

"Sounds disgusting to me," Eddie said, before carefully sipping his hot chocolate. "Besides, do I look like Cupid to you?"

Liza looked at Eddie. He had a chocolate mustache, and chocolate was splattered all over his blue coat. His red baseball cap had snow on the bill and freckles dotted his cheeks. He definitely did *not* look like Cupid.

"Besides," Eddie continued. "Joy is fun and knows how to fix practically everything. She knows all about the hottest toys."

"That's because she gets the inside scoop from Santa," Melody interrupted.

Eddie ignored Melody. "If we help her get back with her husband," Eddie continued, "then she would leave Bailey City. I want her to stay here."

Liza pointed her finger at Eddie. "You can't be selfish about this. Joy deserves to be happy."

"Shh," Melody said. "I think Joy is right behind us."

The kids grew very quiet, except for

Eddie, who slurped the last of his hot chocolate. From the booth behind them, the kids heard Joy talking to Eli. “S.C. is upset,” Eli told Joy. “Nothing has gone right since you left. The workers aren’t organized. The lists are mixed up. There isn’t a single butterscotch drop to be found. There’s no way we can meet our midnight deadline at this rate. You have to come home before it’s too late!”

“Did you hear that?” Liza whispered. “Christmas will be ruined and it will be Eddie’s fault.”

“My fault?” Eddie snapped. “What did I do?”

“You have to choose. Either be selfish or help us save Christmas for everyone,” Liza said. “What will you do?”

11

Love Letter

"I'll help," Melody and Howie said at once. Then all three kids looked at Eddie.

"Okay," Eddie muttered and crushed his hot chocolate cup into a ball. "I'll help."

Liza smiled and leaned close to whisper. "This is what I have in mind. Melody, you're in charge of flowers. Howie, you need to send Joy candy. I'll make a big heart. Eddie, you can write Joy a love letter."

"What?" Eddie shouted. "There's no way I'm going write a l . . . l . . . *l-o-v-e* letter!" Eddie spelled the word so he wouldn't have to say it. He stood up and started to walk way.

Liza looked ready to cry. "You just don't want to help us."

"Eddie never wants to help," Melody said. "He only cares about himself."

"This isn't about friendship. It's about insanity!" Eddie snapped, but he grew quiet when Joy put her hand on his shoulder.

"Is everything all right?" Joy asked.

"Eddie was just talking about a writing a love letter," Melody said with a grin.

A smile formed on Joy's face. "Aren't you kids a little young to be in love?" she asked.

Eddie's face got red all the way to the tips of his ears. He threw his baseball cap on the floor. "I am not in LOVE!" Eddie shouted. Everyone in the restaurant stopped sipping. They quit munching. They stopped talking. They all looked at Eddie. One kid named Ben laughed and started singing, "Eddie's in love! Eddie's in love!"

"Hush," Joy told him. Surprisingly, Ben sat down and got quiet. The rest of the kids went back to talking to their friends.

"Now look what you've done," Eddie fussed at Liza. "Ben will probably tease me for the rest of my life!"

Melody jumped up, put her hands on her hips, and stuck out her jaw. "It's not our fault," she told Eddie. "You're the one who has been acting mean, mean, mean!"

"You're not my friend anymore," Eddie told Melody. "None of you are!"

Liza hopped in front of Eddie before he could leave. "Don't go away mad, Eddie," she said. "We can talk this out. Friendship is too important to waste on a misunderstanding."

Joy nodded her head. "After all," she said, "everyone has arguments, but true friends have to make up and find a way to get along. Friendship isn't always easy, but it's definitely worth saving."

"Joy is right," Liza said. "Friends have to work at getting along. It's the same for husbands and wives. Isn't it, Joy?"

Joy blinked. She opened her mouth,

but no words came out. Eddie knew exactly what had happened. Joy had been tricked into being speechless. Tricked by Liza!

Joy's face turned red. "I need to go and see someone," she finally said. "Liza has reminded me of something very important. I just hope I'm not too late."

"Who do you need to see?" Eddie asked.

"Someone I really love," Joy told the kids. "And it's time I told him so."

Joy hugged each child. "Good-bye!"

"Wait," Liza said, pulling the scarf from around her neck. "Give this to your husband."

"You did it," Howie told Liza after Joy left. "You helped Joy make up with Santa — and Eddie make up with Melody!"

Liza shrugged. "I just hope I wasn't too late. After all, tonight is Christmas Eve."

12

A Package of Proof

Before the kids finished their Doodlegum Shakes, the sky darkened. Thick clouds rolled over Bailey City. Giant snowflakes fell and the wind whipped up snowdrifts.

"We better get home," Howie said. "It looks like we're in for another big snowstorm."

"Aren't you worried?" Melody asked Liza. "What if Santa can't find his way in the snow?"

Liza smiled. "I'm not a bit worried. This snowstorm is the perfect cover for Joy to travel in. I bet she's taking off for the North Pole right now!"

"You never proved that Joy is Mrs. Claus," Eddie said. "And I'm not going to believe it unless you wrap up proof and put it under my Christmas tree!"

Liza didn't argue. Instead, she wished her friends a Merry Christmas and went home.

On Christmas Day, Liza wore new mittens and a hat when she met her friends to go sledding.

Fresh snow had turned the city into a winter wonderland, but Eddie didn't scoop up a single snowball. He didn't kick snow at anyone. He didn't even try to put snow down their backs.

Liza put her hand on Eddie's forehead. "Are you sick?" she asked. "Do you have a fever?"

Eddie shook his head.

"Are you still mad?" Melody asked. "I'm really sorry I teased you yesterday."

"No," Eddie said. "I'm not mad."

"Then what is it?" Howie asked. "You're acting like you didn't get a single present for Christmas."

"I got presents," Eddie finally admitted. "In fact, I got exactly what I wanted — a new, improved, super-duper Zirlot Bug Squasher!"

"That's great," Melody said, jumping up and down in the snow. "Your grandmother must have bought it last July."

Eddie shook his head. "My grandmother didn't give it to me. It didn't come from my dad, either."

"Then who gave it to you?" Howie asked.

"Joy," Eddie said.

Howie laughed and slapped Eddie on the back. "It looks like you got that package of proof you wanted after all!"

Liza grinned and pulled a note from her pocket. "I found a surprise under my tree, too." She read the note out loud. "'Thanks for the scarf.'" It was signed S.C.

"Maybe S.C. really is Santa Claus," Howie shouted.

Melody nodded. "And he's Joy's husband. We saved Christmas after all!"

"If Joy is really Mrs. Claus," Eddie said with a laugh, "then I have to say Santa is one lucky man!"